Lulu
and the Rabbit Next Door

Lulu is a star!

Praise for *Lulu and the Duck in the Park*

2013 ALSC Notable Children's Book

☆☆☆

2013 Book Links Lasting Connection

☆☆☆

2013 Booklist Editors' Choice

☆☆☆

2013 Chicago Public Library Best of the Best

☆☆☆

2012 Kirkus Reviews Best Books of the Year

☆☆☆

2013 USBBY Outstanding International Book List

☆☆☆

2013 CCBC Choice

☆☆☆

2013 ReadKiddoRead Kiddos Finalist

☆☆☆

A Junior Library Guild selection

"McKay shows a rare ability to capture a younger audience in this involving chapter book for transitional readers. The well-structured, third-person narrative builds dramatic tension, provides comic relief of the most believable sort, and shows ***plenty of heart***." —*Booklist* starred review

"A ***warmhearted*** beginning to a new chapter book series delights from the first few sentences…What Lulu and Mellie do to protect the egg, get through class, and not outrage Mrs. Holiday is told so simply and rhythmically and so true to the girls' perfectly-logical-for-third-graders' thinking, that ***it will beguile young readers completely***." —*Kirkus Reviews* starred review

"McKay's pacing is ***spot-on***, and the story moves briskly. Lamont's black-and-white illustrations capture the sparkle in Lulu's eyes and the warmth and fuzziness of a newly hatched duckling. The ***satisfying*** ending will have children awaiting the next installment in what is likely to become a hit series for fans of other plucky characters like Horrible Harry, Stink, and Junie B. Jones." —*School Library Journal* starred review

"Many kids will sympathize with animal-loving Lulu, and McKay's easygoing, perceptive humor adds liveliness to the account…A lighthearted yet eventful outing, this will entice as a chaptery read-aloud as well as a read-alone." —*Bulletin of the Center for Children's Books*

Praise for *Lulu and the Dog from the Sea*

"Whether they live with dogs or not, readers will absorb some truths about family vacations and the true care of animal companions in the company of Lulu and Mellie, who are as **utterly charming** and as completely age seven as possible."—*Kirkus Reviews*

································☆································

"**Fresh as a sea breeze**, the story shows McKay's sure hand in creating characters, both human and canine. A rewarding addition to the Lulu series." —*Booklist*

································☆································

"**McKay hits the nail on the head** in this beginning chapter book…This title should be a staple in any early-chapter-book collection."—*School Library Journal* starred review

································☆································

"Like Lulu's first outing, this is rich in the guileless and eccentric charm that is McKay's hallmark, and the details of a family sorting out the difference between a dream vacation and a real one…will ring true to many readers." —*Bulletin of the Center for Children's Books*, recommended

Praise for *Lulu and the Cat in the Bag*

"This installment in the continuing story of Lulu, her cousin and best friend, Mellie, and her growing collection of pets delights...***It's very funny***." —*Kirkus Reviews*

....☆..

"McKay brings the characters to life in scenes full of warmth, wit, and perception...An appealing beginning chapter book from the excellent Lulu series." —*Booklist*

....☆..

"Another solid entry in this fine series." —*Horn Book*

Look for more books by

Hilary McKay

Lulu and the Duck in the Park

Lulu and the Dog from the Sea

Lulu and the Cat in the Bag

Lulu and the Hedgehog in the Rain

Lulu
and the Rabbit Next Door

Hilary McKay

Illustrated by Priscilla Lamont

Albert Whitman & Company
Chicago, Illinois

Library of Congress Cataloging-in-Publication Data

McKay, Hilary.
Lulu and the rabbit next door / Hilary McKay;
illustrated by Priscilla Lamont.
pages cm
Originally published in the United Kingdom
by Scholastic Children's Books, 2012.
Summary: "When Lulu's next-door neighbor doesn't seem to be looking after his
rabbit properly, Lulu and her cousin Mellie devise a scheme to make him pay
more attention to his pet"—Provided by publisher.
[1. Rabbits—Fiction. 2. Pets—Fiction. 3. Neighbors—Fiction.] I. Lamont,
Priscilla, illustrator. II. Title.
PZ7.M4786574Lv 2014
[Fic]—dc23
2013028645

Text copyright © 2012 by Hilary McKay
Illustrations © 2012 by Priscilla Lamont
First published in the UK by Scholastic Children's Books,
an imprint of Scholastic Ltd.
Published in 2014 by Albert Whitman & Company

ISBN 978-0-8075-4816-5 (hardcover)
ISBN 978-0-8075-4817-2 (paperback)

10 9 8 7 6 5 4 3 2 1 LB 18 17 16 15 14

For more information about Albert Whitman & Company,
visit our web site at www.albertwhitman.com.

To Kaia,
with love from Hot Cat
(and Hilary McKay)

Chapter One

More than Lulu and Mellie Could Bear

All the houses on Lulu's street were very small. "Like Lego houses," said Lulu.

They really did look like toy houses. They had brightly colored doors and flowerpots of flowers and gardens in the back like a row of patchwork squares.

Lulu's house had a green door and a dog's water bowl by the doorstep. Her cousin Mellie, who lived farther down the street, had a yellow door, which she had been allowed to paint herself for a birthday present.

Some people said the street was friendly. Other people said it was nosy. Lulu and Mellie were both friendly and nosy.

At the beginning of summer vacation, when a new family moved into the house next door to Lulu's, they couldn't help watching.

The new family was a father and a mother and a boy. They arrived with a big white van. Lulu and Mellie sat on Lulu's doorstep and watched it being unloaded until Lulu's mother made them come inside.

"It's nice to say hello and be friendly," she told them. "But sitting there staring is too much!"

"We offered to carry things," said Lulu, "but they said no thank you."

"Politely," said Mellie. "They are very polite. And the boy's got an Xbox. We saw it. He carried it in and he didn't come out again."

"He's setting it up," said Lulu. "Let's go and help!"

But Lulu's mother said very firmly that they could not do this either, so they went up to Lulu's room and hung out her window.

That was when they saw that something had appeared in the garden next door.

"A rabbit hutch!" said Lulu, and she hunted out her pirate telescope so she could look at the hutch more closely. "A rabbit hutch *with* a rabbit in it!" she told Mellie triumphantly.

"Why would he have a rabbit hutch without a rabbit in it?" asked Mellie.

"He might have gotten the hutch and be saving up for the rabbit," said Lulu. "I had my hamster cage for ages before I managed to save up for my hamster."

"How old do you think he is?" asked Mellie.

"Older than us," said Lulu. "Eight?"

"Eight?" exclaimed Mellie. "He's not! He was tiny! Six! Six, polite, interested in animals. What else?"

"He'll come out to see his rabbit soon," said Lulu. "Then we'll find out more."

However, the boy did not come out soon. Lulu and Mellie waited a long, long time before he appeared.

"At last!" said Mellie, yawning. She waved, but the boy didn't wave back.

"Shy!" said Mellie.

The boy walked down the garden carrying a bag. He went to the rabbit hutch. He opened the rabbit hutch door. He lifted out a china bowl and filled it with rabbit food out of the bag. He put the bowl back into the hutch and closed the door. Then he hurried back toward the house.

"There's lovely dandelions in his garden," said Lulu. "I wonder if he's noticed."

She called, "Dandelions!" and pointed, but the boy

did not look up. He went inside and he did not appear again. Lulu did not have a chance to talk to him until the next day.

"Hello!" she called.

"I'm busy," said the boy and turned his back.

It was difficult to talk to an unfriendly back, but by trying very hard Lulu managed. And she discovered that everything she and Mellie had guessed the day before was wrong. He wasn't six or eight, he was seven like them. He wasn't shy, and he wasn't at all interested in animals. Lulu found that out by saying, "We saw your rabbit yesterday!"

"Oh," said the boy (his name was Arthur) and shrugged.

"Was he all right, moving house? Not muddled up or anything?"

Arthur turned around then and stared at Lulu as if she were crazy.

"I suppose he'll soon get used to it, anyway," said Lulu. "And he'll like exploring a new garden. There's good dandelions in your garden. There's none left in mine."

"I don't know what you're talking about," said Arthur.

"Dandelions," said Lulu patiently.

"Because I've got two guinea pigs, and they like them just as much as the rabbits. I've got five rabbits. Four who live together because they're friends, and an only rabbit named Thumper who…"

"You've got five rabbits?" demanded Arthur.

Lulu nodded proudly.

"Why would anyone want five boring rabbits?"

"They're *not* boring!"

"I've got one. That's enough. Five! What do you do with five rabbits?"

"Lots of things!"

"Do you know what my one does?"

"What?"

"Nothing!"

"Why did you get him, then?"

"I didn't. My granddad did for my birthday. I told him exactly the game I

wanted for my XBox and he went and got
me a boring rabbit! How fair is that?"

"Why did he?" asked Lulu.

"He says XBoxes are garbage, that's why."

"That's 'cause he's old," said Lulu wisely.

"He's not that old," said Arthur. "He
still plays football! Anyway, he gave me that
rabbit. George. He called it George…"

"Him, not it!" interrupted Lulu.

"It makes no difference!"

"It does! And why don't you give poor
George to someone who does want him?"

"Mom won't let me," said Arthur at once.
"She says Granddad would be upset. And you
don't need to call him poor George! I look
after him. I feed him and I check his water
and I clean him out every single week."

That was true. Lulu knew it was true
because she and Mellie checked. They

could see George's hutch quite clearly from Lulu's bedroom window. With Lulu's telescope they could see George sitting inside.

Day after day.

Week after week.

Twice a day, at breakfast time and dinnertime, Arthur visited George with food and water. Once a week on Saturday mornings, he put him on the ground, scooped all the sawdust out of the hutch into a black trash bag, and put in fresh sawdust. It didn't take long to do this. The whole job was over in just a few minutes.

During those few minutes George became a different rabbit.

A non-sitting rabbit.

He would begin with hops.

Then a stretch.

Then he would begin to run. He ran

faster and faster in
a racing circle all
around the little
garden. Sometimes as he ran,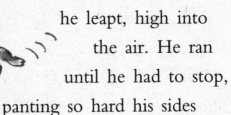

he leapt, high into
the air. He ran
until he had to stop,
panting so hard his sides
went in and out.

Then Arthur would pick him up and
put him back inside his hutch.

To sit there for another week.

It was more than Lulu and Mellie could
bear.

Chapter Two

What Thumper Would Say

Lulu said, "What about kidnapping George?"

"Rabbit-napping," said Mellie.

"Rabbit-napping, then," agreed Lulu.

"Then what?" asked Mellie.

"Rabbit-napping him to my house. And me looking after him."

"But everyone would know he was at your house," objected Mellie.

"How?"

"Lulu!" said Mellie. "Everyone knows

all the animals end up at your house! Your house has animals the way other people's houses have...have...cushions!"

That was not quite true, but it was nearly true. A great many animals did end up at Lulu's house. Some of them, like the hamster who lived in Lulu's bedroom, had been bought by Lulu herself, but most of them had just arrived. Rocko, the bouncy young dog, had been a stray from the beach. Green Ginger, the very old parrot, had belonged to a neighbor who moved away. Four of Lulu's rabbits had come from a rescue center, and the fifth, a fat brown rabbit named Thumper, had been sent from his first home in disgrace.

"We bought him to be a house rabbit," his owners had complained.

Thumper had not known that. No one told him the rules for how house rabbits should behave in houses. *Snip, snip, snip* went his sharp rabbit teeth all in one lively afternoon. They snipped through shoelaces, electric cables, the TV antenna, two laptop chargers, and the telephone line.

"His owners should have been pleased that he wasn't electrocuted!" said Lulu when she heard.

His owners were not pleased. They shut him in the bathroom. Thumper busily dug up a large part of the bathroom floor.

"He is *not* a house rabbit!" said his disappointed owners. "He is a problem rabbit!" They gave him to Lulu, who gave him twigs to snip instead of cables and earth to dig in instead of bathroom floors. He was still a bit of a problem rabbit, though. The other rabbits would not be friends with him. They chased him away when he thumped over to them to play.

"If I rabbit-napped George, he could be Thumper's friend," said Lulu, but Mellie would not agree. She had a much better idea.

"Better! Braver! More exciting!" she said, bouncing as she spoke. "Arthur keeps poor George in a cage with nothing to do, doesn't he?"

"Yes," agreed Lulu.

"So what we should do is put Arthur in a cage with nothing to do!"

"Why…"

"Then he would see what it's like!"

"But…"

"Your shed could be the cage! We could take out the guinea pigs because they make it too interesting and Arthur could sleep on those bags of hay. And we could feed him food through the window. Boring food. Very plain sandwiches. Admit my idea is ten million times better than yours!"

But Lulu would not admit this. She said Mellie's idea was ten million times worse. "For one thing," said Lulu, "there isn't a toilet in the shed!"

"Who cares?" said Mellie.

"You can't just say who cares!" said Lulu. "Think about it!"

But Mellie would not think about it. She just kept saying how good her idea was compared to Lulu's. For several days they argued, and all the time George sat in his hutch.

And then something happened.

Arthur knocked on Lulu's door, and he said, "We're going on vacation."

"Oh," said Lulu, and then, to be a little more polite, she added, "That's nice."

"Yes, but there's my rabbit," said Arthur.

"George," said Lulu.

"It can't come."

"He, not it!"

"He," said Arthur. "That's what I meant. So could you look after it? Him. *Him?* You know who I mean! George! Could you? It's dead easy. You don't need to bother to clean him out because we're only going away for a week. All you have to do is come by and feed him and check he's got some water."

"That's not how you look after rabbits!" said Lulu.

"Yes, it is," said Arthur, sounding very surprised.

"Well, it's not how I look after rabbits!" said Lulu. "But I will look after George. Not at your house, though. He can have his hutch close to Thumper's and they can make friends."

When Mellie saw George at Lulu's house, she thought Lulu had done rabbit-napping without her and she got very mad and said it wasn't fair.

"No, no, no, *listen*!" said Lulu. "George has come on vacation to here because Arthur went on vacation to the seaside."

"*Oh!*" said Mellie, suddenly under-standing. Then she said hopefully, "Perhaps he'll stay there forever!"

"And leave his XBox?"
asked Lulu.

"He wouldn't do
that," Mellie admitted.

"Unless
he took
it," said
Lulu. "I
bet he
did!
And
he'll probably
stay in his bedroom XBoxing for
the whole vacation and not even see the
sea! But who cares! We've got George!
Let's get him out of that hutch!"

That was the beginning of a wonderful
week for George.

He learned to dig.

He learned his name.

He learned to race a tennis ball.

He made friends with Thumper and they went exploring together.

He found how nice it was to stretch in the sun.

And leave footprints in the dew.

And reach up high to nibble a leaf.

His fur was brushed.

His nails were clipped.

His eyes watched brightly for the next interesting thing to happen.

And then he went home.

Arthur didn't say hello to George when he came to collect him. He didn't ask if he had been happy. He didn't notice how sad Lulu was. He didn't say thank you to her either, but he gave her a box of fudge.

"Thank you," said Lulu.

"My mom bought it, not me," said Arthur.

On the lid of the box it said, *A Little Present for Taking Care of my Dog/Cat/Pet.* You were supposed to check which one it was, but Arthur hadn't bothered. After that there was a space where you were supposed to write the name of the animal that had been taken care of. Arthur hadn't done that either.

"School on Monday," said Lulu, just for something to say, because she felt so awkward holding the unbothered-with box of fudge and at the same time trying not to cry.

"Yeah," said Arthur.

"You'll be in my class."

Arthur shrugged.

"You don't have to take George home right now if you don't want to," said Lulu suddenly. "You can leave him here for as long as you like."

"No thanks," said Arthur, and he picked up one end of George's hutch and began bumping him up the garden path.

George leapt in alarm and Lulu rushed to the hutch and pulled open the door and grabbed him.

"Put him back!" said Arthur indignantly.

"No!" said Lulu, hugging George.

"Put him back *now*!"

"I'll carry him for you. You bring the hutch. I'll bring George."

"Who do you think you're bossing?"

"I'm not bossing, I'm helping," said Lulu, and she ran ahead with George so that Arthur had to follow whether he liked it or not.

"Thank you for *nothing!*" said Arthur when he caught up with them both. Then he grabbed back George, pushed him into his hutch, slammed shut the door, and marched inside. He didn't come out again all that day.

Or the next day.

Neither did George.
Lulu and Mellie behaved very badly about the box of fudge. They kicked it around the garden like a football.

"*Now* we definitely have to kidnap Arthur!" said Mellie, kicking the box of fudge against the shed.

"Now we definitely have to rabbit-nap George!" said Lulu, and she kicked the box against the fence so hard that it burst open. A piece of fudge shot out and just missed Thumper's nose. He jumped in

surprise and Lulu and
Mellie stopped being
angry and became
sorry instead.

"Poor Thumper!"
said Lulu, sitting
beside him and
rubbing him in his favorite place to be
rubbed, which was just behind his ears.
"Help me think what to do, Mellie!
Kidnapping won't work. Rabbit-napping
won't work. Being mad doesn't work.
What will?"

Mellie sat down on the other side of
Thumper and ate a piece of squashed fudge
while she thought. She said, "I wonder
what Thumper would say."

Lulu found herself a square of fudge. She
wiped off the mud and ate it slowly. She
said, "Thumper will miss George."

"If they had phones, they could talk to each other," said Mellie.

"Or text," said Lulu.

"Or email if they had computers," said Mellie, reaching over Thumper for the fudge that had just missed his nose.

"They could write!" said Lulu.

"What?"

"They could write," repeated Lulu. "Are you sitting on any more fudge, Thumper? Yes! Good!"

"Thumper and George could write?"

"Thumper could, anyway," said Lulu. "He could write to George. He could send messages over the fence."

"Could he?"

"Why not?"

"What would he say?"

"He would say...he would say...Dear George..."

Chapter Three

Dear George

It took some time for the girls to arrange everything. First they had to make plans. Then there was the fence. It was too high to climb quickly. They had to find flowerpots and boxes to make steps. And of course, they had to go to school as well. But at last:

Dear George,
   I hope you are well.
   I have had a very busy day.
   Lulu emptied my hutch and threw

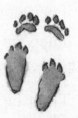

everything away. She even threw away my
lovely bed. She gave me new hay to make
a new bed. She did not help at all. She
stuffed all the new hay in a paper bag and
I had to unpack it and make another bed all
by myself. It took ages and ages and ages.
   Your very tired friend, Thumper

   P.S. I am sending you a bag of hay
so you can see for yourself what hard work
it was.

This message appeared on top of George's
hutch early one morning, balanced on top
of a large bag of hay.

Arthur stared at it.

Then at George.

Then up at Lulu's house to see if anyone
was watching.

Then he read the message again.

George scrabbled impatiently at the wire of his hutch.

Arthur did not believe a rabbit would know what to do with a bag of hay. He thought it was a trick.

He checked again to see if anyone was watching, staring suspiciously up at Lulu's window. He listened for the sound of someone in the garden next door.

"No one," he said aloud.

George looked at him. His look asked, *How much longer?*

Very quickly, as if he was doing something wrong, Arthur opened George's door and pushed the bag of hay inside.

After that, Arthur hurried back indoors, but before he set off for school that morning he checked on George.

George had his head in the bag. He was very busy. He looked like he knew exactly what to do with a bag of hay.

That morning Arthur caught up with Lulu and Mellie as they all went into class together. He said, "I know it's you! I'm not stupid!"

Lulu and Mellie looked at each other. Mellie rolled her eyes. Lulu shrugged. Their looks said, *What is the matter with this boy?*

Arthur went very red and said crossly, "Rabbits can't write!"

"Parrots can talk," said Lulu helpfully.

"Whales can sing," said Mellie.

"Squirrels can fly," added Lulu. "Some of them, anyway. Tigers can swim."

"So can fish," said Mellie.

"Fish can do lots of things," said Lulu. "Jump! And make nests. Like gorillas."

"*Gorillas!*" shouted Arthur.

"Giraffes," said Mellie, "can't cough. It said so on Animal Planet. What about when they have sore throats?"

"I hope they don't," said Lulu.

"Nan says cats can walk through walls," said Mellie.

"Beavers can definitely chew through trees," said Lulu.

"You are crazy!" growled Arthur.

"Who?" asked Lulu. "Me or Mellie? Mellie is a little crazy. She's saving up for a hot air balloon. Where's she going to put it? She's only got a little bedroom."

"I've told you and told you," said Mellie. "I'll tie it to the roof. There's plenty of space in the sky. Lulu's a little crazy. She jumps off swings when they're swinging. Very dangerous."

"Only for a moment," said Lulu.

"When you land!" said Mellie.

"You're *both* crazy!" snapped Arthur. "And you think you are so clever and everything you say is made up!"

"Nothing I said was made up," said Lulu.

"Nothing I said was made up either," said Mellie. "Especially about the hot air balloon!"

"Lulu, Mellie, and Arthur!" called Mrs. Holiday, the not-very-patient teacher of Class Three. "I am about to take attendance so kindly stop yattering! Whatever is all the argy-bargy about, anyway?"

(Long before, Mrs. Holiday had lived in Scotland, where she had learned many strange and interesting words. Class Three had learned them too. *Argy-bargy* was one of them.)

"It is an argy-bargy about rabbits," Mellie told Mrs. Holiday.

"Oh, rabbits!" said Mrs. Holiday, and she looked carefully at Lulu and said, "Lulu, I trust you have no livestock hidden on the premises today?"

Lulu understood that this was Mrs. Holiday's way of asking if she had any dogs in the playground or hamsters in her pocket

or ducklings under her sweater,
all things that had
happened at school
in the past.

She shook her
head.

"No, Mrs. Holiday," she said. "Not
today."

Mrs. Holiday looked at Mellie.

Mellie's eyes were wide with innocence.

"No rabbits or anything," she said.

"Arthur?" asked Mrs. Holiday with her eyebrows raised high.

"What?" asked Arthur, now in a complete temper. "Me? Why'd I want to bring a boring rabbit to school? No, thank you! Or a boring giraffe or a boring parrot or a boring…"

Arthur suddenly stopped and glared around at the listening class.

"Yes?" asked Mrs. Holiday.

"Gorilla," said Arthur very sulkily indeed, and the whole class collapsed with laughter.

"Well," said Mrs. Holiday, who was always kind to people who were new. "No gorillas. Excellent. Very good news! Now then, everyone, times tables!"

Times tables cheered up Arthur because he was very good at math, and they cured Lulu and Mellie's giggles entirely because they weren't.

For the rest of that school day Lulu and Mellie did not see much of Arthur. They kept out of his way because he looked at them so crossly. But he caught up with them on the way home. They were in the little park at the end of their street where they sometimes stopped to swing.

Arthur seemed ready to start the whole argybargy all over again. He glared up at Lulu and Mellie as they sailed backward and forward.

"Rabbits *can't* write!" he said.

"I can fly," said Lulu, and she let go of her swing at its highest point and soared in a lovely curve through the air.

A moment later she was rolling in pain on the muddy grass.

"As usual!" groaned Mellie, stopping her own swing so she could hurry to the rescue. "Is it your knees again?"

"My ankle!" said Lulu. "Ow! Ow! Ow!

Never mind! Did you see how far I went?
Wasn't it great?"

"No, it wasn't!" said Mellie. "It was
crazy! Now you're going to have to hop all
the way home. Can you carry her bag for
her, Arthur?"

"Can't you?" asked Arthur grumpily.

"Yes, if you'll help Lulu."

"No, I won't. I'll carry the bag," said
Arthur, and he picked it up while Mellie

heaved Lulu to her feet. For the rest of the way home he and Mellie walked on each side of her and took turns to tell her how silly she was. Arthur seemed to enjoy this, in the same way that he had enjoyed the times tables that morning.

"I know, I know, I know, I know," said Lulu, who had heard it all before.

At home Lulu was told off some more, and had a bag of frozen peas tied around her sore ankle. This had also happened before. And then it was dinnertime and homework time and play with the animals time and then, just when she had gone up to her bedroom with an armload of carrots and sticks and string, Mellie came puffing up the stairs.

"Good. You can help," said Lulu. "I'm making carrot mobiles for the rabbits."

"I didn't come to help," said Mellie.
"I came because I've thought of something
awful! What if your ankle isn't better
by tomorrow?"

"It will be better," said Lulu, stretching
out her vegetable-bandaged foot. "It's
getting better all the time. It had peas
before dinner, and it's got sweet corn now,
and if that doesn't work there's
some frozen Brussels sprouts

from last Christmas! You are going to help, aren't you? I need lots of little carrot chunks tied on like beads."

Mellie, who had helped make carrot mobiles before, reached for string and carrots and looked worriedly at Lulu's foot.

"Last time you did it, you had to miss PE for a week," she said. "And it was the week Charlie had chicken pox and we had dance and Mrs. Holiday made me have Henry for a partner. It's dance tomorrow!"

"Yes, but Charlie doesn't have chicken pox now," said Lulu, munching a carrot.

"I know, but what if this time she makes me dance with Arthur!"

"He wouldn't like that much," said Lulu cheerfully.

"He wouldn't like it!" repeated Mellie. "What about me? Stop eating carrots and show me your foot!"

"Carrots are good for you," said Lulu, but all the same she stopped eating them and unwrapped her foot. "See! Perfect!" she said.

"It's swollen," complained Mellie, prodding it with a carrot.

"Ouch! It's not! Only a little."

"I will have to dance with Arthur!" said Mellie. "It's all your fault! Admit it's all your fault!"

"I admit it," said Lulu cheerfully. "But it can't be worse than dancing with Henry. Anyway, it might not happen. I'm getting better every minute."

"Really?"

"Every second," said Lulu. "I promise. And look!"

She held up a finished mobile, bright chains of carrots swinging from sticks. "That will keep George busy for ages," she said.

"When are you going to give it to him?"

"Early in the morning, over the fence."

Mellie looked at Lulu's ankle.

"And how will Arthur know what it is?"

"He'll read this letter. It's a message from Thumper."

"Show it to me!" commanded Mellie.

Lulu passed over a sheet of cardboard covered in careful rabbit writing, Thumper's latest message to George. Mellie frowned over it, chewing a spare mobile stick while she thought.

"Even if you get it over the fence and even if Arthur understands what a carrot mobile is, you can't be certain he'll hang it up for George," she said at last. "You'd better put a P.S. to be sure. Can I write it? Because I've thought of something perfect."

Lulu passed Mellie her pencil.

Mellie turned Thumper's letter over and wrote.

Lulu read what she had written, hopped across the room, and hugged her.

"That's perfect!" she said.

Chapter Four

Anything Is Better than Boring

It looked like rubbish to Arthur. A messy heap of sticks and string and chunks of carrot. It didn't swing into shape until he lifted it up and then he read the message underneath.

Dear George,
    Here is a carrot mobile to decorate your hutch.
    Lots of love from Thumper

"A carrot mobile!" said Arthur aloud. "What kind of stupid thing is a carrot mobile?" He would have thrown it away right then if the message had not happened to flutter to the ground. Then he saw that there was writing on the back:

You're going to need someone really brainy to hang it up for you!

So that meant, as Arthur understood at once, that the carrot mobile had to be hung up. Unless he was not brainy enough.

It was hard to fix. Impossible with George there, bouncy and eager. In the end Arthur put him on the ground while he tied the sticks into place. It took so long that he had to rush to do all the other things that needed doing before school: eat breakfast, brush his teeth, find his school bag, hug his mom, duck the comb she had seized, catch George and put him back in his hutch, forget his jacket...

"Run!" called his mother, waving from the doorstep, and Arthur ran so fast that once again he caught up with Lulu and Mellie as they headed into the classroom.

Lulu's foot was not better, even despite the Brussels sprouts. She had a pink bandage around her ankle and a note for Mrs. Holiday saying please could she rest it for the day.

"Really, Lulu!" said Mrs. Holiday. "When will you learn to be sensible?"

"If there was a great big trampoline in front of the swings it wouldn't happen," said Lulu.

"Yes, but there *isn't* a great big trampoline in front of the swings!" said Mrs. Holiday. "So why can't you just sit still, Lulu, like everybody else?"

"Just sitting is boring," said Lulu. "Just sitting there when you could jump!"

She smiled up at Mrs. Holiday, trying to make her understand.

"Anything is better than boring," she said.

Mellie was jiggling with impatience.

"Mrs. Holiday!" she said. "What about dance? 'Cause Lulu's my partner. Couldn't we do it another day instead?"

"Not at all!" said Mrs. Holiday in her most Scottish voice. "Another day indeed! Why in the world would we do that? And you needn't worry, Mellie, because here is Arthur all ready and waiting for a partner!"

The class giggled. Lulu looked sadly at her bandage. Mellie and Arthur turned away from each other with equal dismay. Mrs. Holiday took no notice. She liked teaching dance, especially the dances she had learned herself at school. "Lulu can clap and learn to call the figures!" she said.

So that was what happened, and above the cheerful sounds of Scottish music Mrs. Holiday and Lulu clapped and called:

"Greet your partners!" Mrs. Holiday murmured to Lulu.

"Greet your partners!" called Lulu.

"All take hands! (Louder this time, Lulu!)"

"ALL TAKE HANDS!"

"(Much better!) Form a circle!"

"FORM A CIRCLE!"

"Eight skips right!"

"EIGHT SKIPS RIGHT!"

Mellie and Arthur, since they had been forced to be partners, livened up the dance by squabbling in time to the music.

"Can't you count?"

"*Don't* keep stopping!"

"She said right!"

"This *is* right!"

"Who put that stuff on George's hutch? I bet it was you because of her foot!"

"Wrong then, ha ha! And not that way! You've got to swing everyone all down the line!"

BOING!

That was the chord at the end of the music. Mellie and Arthur sprang apart like two magnets that had been pushed together the wrong way.

"THANK YOUR PARTNERS!" called Lulu and Mrs. Holiday. "And BOW!"

"I'm never doing that again as long as I live!" said Arthur, bowing to Mellie.

"I'm not either so don't change your mind!" said Mellie, bowing beautifully back.

The carrot mobile had almost vanished by the time Arthur got home that afternoon. Only one slice remained, swinging above

George's head. As Arthur watched, George stretched, caught it, and munched it up. He did it so neatly that Arthur laughed out loud.

"Hello!" called a friendly voice, and there was Lulu's mother on the other side of the fence. "Good day at school?"

"I had to dance with Mellie."

"I know. She told me."

"What did she say?"

"She said you were a thousand times better than Henry."

Arthur was so surprised and pleased that his mouth fell open. Lulu's mother laughed.

"Thank you for helping Lulu home last night. I don't know what she's thinking of, jumping like that! Very silly!"

"Yes," agreed Arthur, but he did not say it as if he meant it. The surprised, pleased feeling was still there. He was no longer quite sure what he thought of Lulu and Mellie.

After Lulu's mother had gone, Arthur looked again at George. He couldn't help remembering what Lulu had said as she hopped in front of Mrs. Holiday. "Anything is better than boring" and "Just sitting there, when you could jump."

"Go on then," he said to George and lifted him down into the garden.

Chapter Five

Love from Thumper

Dear George,
    This is a parcel for YOU to unwrap.
    Lots of love from Thumper

It was a lumpy package nearly as big as
George, wrapped in brown paper and tied
with string.

Very carefully, as if it might explode,
Arthur picked it up.

George watched.

Arthur tugged at the string.

George looked shocked.

Arthur looked at the letter again.

for YOU to unwrap

Arthur opened the door of George's hutch and delivered the parcel.

All at once George became very awake. He hopped round his parcel, inspecting it from all sides. He sniffed it carefully. He rubbed his chin over the knot in the string. He scrabbled at it with his paws, rolling it over.

Arthur wondered if he should help.

Then George picked the whole parcel up in his teeth, holding it by the string. He shook his head.

Suddenly the string popped open and the brown paper became loose.

"Hey, well done!" said Arthur.

But inside the parcel was another parcel, just the same. More string. More paper.

"What a cheat!" said Arthur indignantly. "Poor old George! Give it to me!"

He reached into the hutch and took out the parcel. A large yellow dandelion flower fell from the wrappings. It must have been between the layers, like the sweets hidden between the layers of a party pass-the-parcel. George pounced on it at once.

He looked very funny eating the
dandelion. At first it fluffed out of his
mouth like a bright yellow cloud. Then,
bit by bit, bite by bite, it disappeared. A
few yellow petals dropped onto the hay.
George sniffed them out and ate them too.

Arthur remembered something Lulu had
said. He looked around the garden. Sure
enough, dandelions everywhere. He picked
the biggest he could find and gave it to
George.

"Now I've got to go and have my
breakfast," he told him.

George looked hopefully at his parcel.

"Sorry," said Arthur and gave it back.

When Arthur went to check on George
just before school, George had unwrapped
another layer. He was sitting on the paper
chewing a radish. Between his paws was

the parcel, just the same but slightly smaller. George looked very bright-eyed and busy. Arthur picked him another dandelion and went to school looking thoughtful.

Often during the day Arthur thought of George with his parcel. He wondered what was the middle. As soon as he got home that afternoon he hurried into the garden to find out. There was George, sitting on top of an enormous pile of screwed-up paper, string, and hay, gnawing up the last of a sweet potato.

"You'll get fat!" said Arthur, lifting him to the ground. "You'd better go for a run!"

George raced round the garden with jumps higher than ever. Watching him, Arthur was impressed. He thought, *If I could jump as well as George I could jump over…I could jump over…street signs! Mail boxes! I could jump over cars!*

How cool would it be, thought Arthur, *if on the way to school I could do that!*

"Even just once would be fantastic!" he told George. "You're lucky! You can do it every day!"

George stopped running and looked at Arthur.

Arthur looked at George.

"If I let you," admitted Arthur.

But things were changing for George.
Every day there was a new surprise.

A bundle of twigs labeled, **Apple Twigs!
Bite to bits!** and a notice for the garden gate:

**PLEASE KEEP CLOSED!
RABBIT IN THE GARDEN!**

Another parcel and a very grumbly letter
from Thumper.

Dear George,

Today has been a very bad day.

First they cut my nails with their special
nail cutter thing.

Then they brushed me and brushed me
with their hairbrush thing.

🦋 65 🦋

Then they put STUFF BEHIND MY EARS.

Ear cream.

Just where I cannot lick it off.

They say the stuff is to keep away flies.

What flies?

I do not have flies.

Love from your much too

clean and tidy friend, Thumper

P.S. Here is some horrible ear cream so that you can see what it's like.

P.S. again. And here is that tennis ball you used to like to chase.

George was just as cross as Thumper had been when Arthur put the ear cream behind his ears. But Lulu and Mellie, watching through cracks in the fence, were very pleased indeed. And they nudged each other with delight when after

Mellie nodded.

"Perhaps we won't have to rabbit-nap George after all!"

"No," agreed Mellie. "Or kidnap Arthur and lock him in the shed." Mellie sighed. "I suppose that's good," she said, but she didn't sound like she thought it was good. She sounded disappointed. Since she and Arthur had been such a good dance team she had looked forward more than ever to keeping Arthur like a pet in the shed.

"Even just for an afternoon it would have been good," she said. "It would have been exciting."

"We'll do something else exciting," said Lulu. "I've been thinking."

"What?"

"Arthur's gotten much better, hasn't he? He's a lot nicer to George, and he's been really friendly lately…"

"We've tamed him," said Mellie. "Almost."

"Yes," agreed Lulu. "So do you think he might bring George around to visit Thumper this weekend?"

Mellie thought and then shook her head.

"No. He's not that tame yet."

"I don't want George and Thumper to forget about each other," said Lulu worriedly.

"Perhaps he might for something special. If he was invited."

"Like for a party?"

"Perhaps."

"We'll have one, then! A birthday party!"

"But it's nobody's birthday," objected Mellie.

"Thumper's!" said Lulu triumphantly.

"Is it?"

"It might be," said Lulu. "It must be! Think how long I've had him! And he's never had a birthday while he's lived with me. I don't suppose he had one before he came here either. So it must be very nearly his birthday. In fact, it's probably almost exactly his birthday…"

"Today?" asked Mellie, very surprised.

"Not today," said Lulu. "Today would be too late to arrange anything. Tomorrow! That's when Thumper can have his birthday!"

"I didn't get him a present," said Mellie, suddenly worried.

"Neither did I, but we will."

"And a birthday cake?"

"Yes, a carrot cake."

"And he's having a party?"

"With all his friends."

"But there's only George!"

"I know. So we'd better hurry up and send him an invitation."

Chapter Six

A Perfect Present

Dear George,

Please come to my birthday party tomorrow because tomorrow is probably my birthday.

It is at three o'clock.

Love from Thumper

P.S. It is not one of those parties where you don't bring presents.

Lulu and Mellie put in the P.S. because

there was an awful new fashion at their school for parties without presents. They would not have put it in if they'd known how much it would alarm Arthur.

Arthur had gotten into the habit of rolling out of bed and heading straight for George's hutch, and so he found the party invitation almost as soon as it had been delivered. The invitation was written on

ordinary paper, but its envelope was made from cabbage leaves sewn together with long grasses.

Arthur read the message while George ate the envelope.

Not one of those parties where you don't bring presents.

Arthur's pocket money was spent. His money box was empty.

And even if this was not so, even if his pockets and money box were stuffed full of five-dollar bills, he still wouldn't know what to buy a rabbit like Thumper.

"Thumper has everything already," he grumbled to George. "This is going to be awful!" He looked at the invitation and added, "I wish I'd stayed in bed."

At Lulu's house the party preparations had already begun. Lulu's mother said she was very happy to make a carrot cake

birthday cake for Thumper if Lulu and
Mellie would help by measuring the flour
and sugar and cinnamon, and grating the
carrots, and breaking the eggs, and then
mixing everything together with a little
orange juice.

And putting it in the cake pan.

And clearing up the floury sugary eggy splashes they had made.

And reminding her to put it in the oven.

And reminding her to take it out again.

The rest of the party food was much more simple.

"Salad and cookies," said Lulu, and Mellie agreed that everyone invited, human or animal, would probably eat salad and cookies.

Also there were party bags to be filled with homemade popcorn and party games to be decided.

The games were:

First rabbit up the stairs.

Hide-and-seek in Lulu's bedroom (where the last rabbit found would be the winner).

Musical Radishes, which Lulu said would be just like musical chairs, except instead of taking away a chair they would take away a radish.

The Big Dig (or race to the bottom of the sandbox).

"And if we have time and everyone wants, the dogs will do their Dog Talent Show!" said Lulu.

"Um," said Mellie, who had seen the dogs' talent show many times before. "Oh well. Perhaps Arthur and George will think it's funny. If they come."

"If they come?"

"Well, they haven't said they will. We should have put that thing on the invitation."

"What thing?"

"Those letters that mean you've got to say if you're coming," explained Mellie. "Or not!"

Lulu could not bear the thought of not. "But the carrot cake is baking and we've made the party bags!" she protested. "They've got to come!"

"I suppose we could ask," said Mellie doubtfully. "Say, 'Are you coming or not?' But then Arthur would know it was us as well as Thumper."

"What was us as well as Thumper?"

"You know. The messages and the presents and the party invitation!"

Lulu knew not to ask, "Do you really believe he doesn't know it's us?" She knew her crazy, lovely friend Mellie very well. Mellie could believe in lots of things that other people could not: her own rooftop hot air balloon, for instance, and the way she seemed to go slightly invisible when she closed her eyes.

Lulu thought it would be a pity if Mellie stopped believing things. So she said, "We won't ask. We'll just have to guess that they'll come. If they don't, we'll...we'll—"

"We'll go and get them!" said Mellie. "And you can rabbit-nap George for the party and I'll really put Arthur in the shed! That'll teach him what it's like to be kept in a hutch when you're supposed to be at a party! Lulu, what about Thumper's birthday presents?"

Arthur had avoided the present problem by going back to bed with his XBox. When his mom came to see where he was, she found him surrounded by banana peels and cookie wrappers, hacking up *Star Wars* enemies with his light saber.

He said, "If anyone comes for me, will you tell them I'm sick?"

"Are you sick?" asked his mother, looking crossly at the banana peels and other mess.

"Well, will you tell them I'm busy?" asked Arthur, zapping things very quickly and not looking up at her. "Too busy to do anything."

"Too busy?" asked his mom.

"Yes," said Arthur, turning up the volume on his game.

"For goodness' sake!" exclaimed his mom. "Turn that down!"

"What?"

"Turn it down! In fact, turn the silly thing *off* and get out of bed! It's almost lunchtime! And you can tidy up this mess and go outside and clean out that rabbit!"

"I will later."

Arthur's mother did the terrible thing she sometimes did. She pulled out the XBox plug.

Then she stepped over a banana peel and marched out of the room looking scary.

Arthur got up very slowly.

He had a very long shower.

He cleared up his bedroom more carefully than he had ever cleared it before.

He plugged in his XBox again, very quietly, with no sound at all, was caught by his mother, and was chased outside.

Outside he felt a little bit better. Lulu and Mellie were not around and George was very pleased to see him.

"Yes, but what about this party?" Arthur asked him, as he dumped him on the ground.

George skipped about in a partyish sort of way.

"We've got to bring a present!" Arthur reminded him.

George stopped skipping and looked up at Arthur. A look that said, *Well! Where's the present?*

"I don't have one and I can't think of one," said Arthur.

George looked like a rabbit who was trying to think.

"Don't say carrots because I expect he's got millions," said Arthur. "Don't say cabbages either! Or things to chew! Or carrot mobiles or pass-the-parcels or notices for the gate! Lulu's thought of all those things already."

George picked up a stray strand of hay and nibbled it.

"Or hay," said Arthur. "He's got plenty of hay."

Then George did something so amazing, so clever, so just right, that at first Arthur could only stare. And then he ran inside and dragged his mother into the garden, and all in a rush of words he gabbled out the story of Thumper and George, and the messages and the parcels, and the party invitation and finally the terrible birthday-present problem that had sent him back to bed. And he said, "Look at George! Look at George! Look at George!"

But Arthur's mother was already looking at George.

Then she and Arthur and George as well all became terribly busy.

It was a wonderful party!

George won first rabbit upstairs.

Hide-and-seek in Lulu's bedroom turned into the Great escape from Lulu's bedroom and then hide-and-seek all over the house.

Musical Radishes did not work well because all the players took no notice of the music and insisted on eating the radishes instead of running around them.

The Big Dig emptied the sandbox.

George won that game too. Lulu looked at Thumper to see if he minded losing twice at his own birthday party. He and George were busy washing each other's sandy faces. It was easy to see that Thumper did not mind a bit.

Salad and cookies and carrot cake made a perfect birthday lunch.

Everyone helped blow out the candles on the carrot cake, and everyone made a wish.

Lulu forgot about the Dog Talent Show and Mellie did not remind her.

And then it was time for Thumper to open his birthday presents.

Lulu's mother gave him a Weetabix.

Lulu gave him a large red rose. (Thumper loved red roses. He gobbled them up much faster than all the other colors.)

Mellie's present was a picture of his

friend George, drawn with chalk on the
wall of his hutch.

But Arthur and George's present was
huge and beautiful. A
flowerpot tied with
a yellow ribbon
and planted full of
dandelions.

"Dandelions!"
exclaimed Lulu
and Mellie and
Lulu's mother.
"What a perfect
present!"

Arthur smirked.
He knew it was a
perfect present. He had
known for hours.

"George thought of it!" he told
everyone. "He thought of it and he dug

up the first dandelion and then he helped
me and Mom find lots more. I dug
them up and Mom planted them. She
tied on that ribbon too. You can take it
off if you like. But it was all George's
idea first!"

"George is clever," said Mellie.
"Thumper is too. Think of all the letters
he wrote…" She paused and looked at
Arthur under her eyelashes, but Arthur
only grinned and did not protest. "…
But George is very clever! He must have
noticed Thumper didn't have dandelions
when he stayed here that week. And he
remembered all
that time!"

Arthur looked proudly at George, who
was sharing Thumper's rose. Then he went
on to tell Lulu and Mellie more interesting
things about his rabbit.

How he knew not only his name, but
Thumper's name too, and would gaze in
the direction of Thumper's house whenever
he heard it.

How he had begun to dig a burrow.

How, after the dandelions had been planted,
they had both gone inside to wash the mud
off before the party, and how George had
jumped on Arthur's bed.

"So I thought I'd show him my XBox,"

said Arthur. "And he loved it. 'Specially *Star Wars*. I'm going to start again at the first level so he can follow it properly."

"Lucky George," said Mellie enviously.

"You can come too," offered Arthur.

"All of us? Thumper as well?" asked Lulu.

"If you like," said Arthur.

Lulu and Mellie looked at each other. And then they looked at Arthur. They looked at him as proudly as he had looked at George.

Arthur did not notice. He was lying on his stomach on Lulu's bedroom floor. Rabbits were climbing on him. He was eating dandelions.

Lulu wished she could say something to show how pleased she was. How quickly he had changed. How nice he had turned out to be. But she could not think of anything until Arthur spoke himself.

"One day," said Arthur, "when it's George's birthday, could Thumper come for a sleepover? I'd look after him. Would you let him?"

Then Lulu knew what to say.

"'Course I would," said Lulu.

Look for more

Lulu

adventures!

weep!

Lulu and the Duck in the Park
HC 978-0-8075-4808-8
$13.99
PB 978-0-8075-4809-7
$4.99

When Lulu finds a duck egg that has rolled out of its nest, she takes it to class to keep it safe. Lulu isn't allowed to bring pets to school. But she's not really breaking the rules. It's just an egg, after all. Surely nothing bad will happen…

......................................☆......................................

"'Lulu was famous for animals,' opens this **sparkling** series launch…This offering has…**abundant humor and heart**."—*Publishers Weekly* starred review

......................................☆......................................

"McKay introduces complex characters, and animal-loving Lulu's dilemma **rings true**."—*Horn Book* starred review

Lulu and the Dog from the Sea
HC 978-0-8075-4820-2
$13.99
PB 978-0-8075-4821-9
$4.99

When Lulu goes on vacation, she finds a dog living on the beach. Everyone in the town thinks the dog is trouble. But Lulu is sure he just needs a friend. And that he's been waiting for someone just like her...

Lulu and the Cat in the Bag
HC 978-0-8075-4804-2
$13.99
PB 978-0-8075-4805-9
$4.99

When a mysterious bag is left on Lulu's doorstep, the last thing her nan expects to be in it is a cat—a huge, marigold-colored cat. But Lulu knows this cat doesn't mean any harm and in fact it needs a lovely new home.

Lulu and the Hedgehog in the Rain
978-0-8075-7812-7
$13.99

When Lulu rescues a hedgehog in a storm, she knows
she can't keep it as a pet—hedgehogs are wild animals
that want to roam free. But can Lulu find a way to keep
the hedgehog safe?

About the Author

Hilary McKay is the eldest of four girls and grew up in a household of readers. After studying zoology and botany in college, Hilary went on to work as a biochemist. She became a full-time mother and writer after the birth of her two children. Hilary says one of the best things about being a writer is receiving letters from children. Hilary now lives in a small village in England with her family. When not writing, she loves walking, reading, and having friends over to visit.